to Issy, Ed, Theo, Ruby, Grace and Tom

SIMON AND SCHUSTER

Published in 2004 by Simon & Schuster UK Ltd
Africa House, 64-78 Kingsway, London WC2B 6AH.

Originally published in 2004 by Atheneum Books for Young Readers,
an imprint of Simon & Schuster Children's Publishing Division, New York.

This paperback edition published in 2004.

Text and illustrations copyright © 2004 Alan Snow.

The right of Alan Snow to be identified as the author and illustrator of this work has been
asserted by him in accordance with the Copyright, Designs and Patents Act, 1988.

Book designed by Polly Kanevsky.
The text for this book is set in Lomba.
The illustrations for this book are rendered in pen and ink, with digital colour.

A CIP catalogue record for this book is available from the British Library upon request .

ISBN-10: 1-416-90150-7
ISBN-13: 978-1-4169-0150-1
Printed in China
8 10 9

Where does Santa live?

Santa (or Father Christmas, as he is also known) lives under the North Pole. He has a small, comfortable home beneath the snow and ice. Each morning after he wakes up he gets out of bed, has a bath, gets dressed, makes breakfast and then goes downstairs to start work.

Where does Santa work?

Beneath his living quarters is everything he needs to make Christmas happen. There are factories, warehouses, transport facilities, a communications centre and many other vital and necessary departments. This book covers all these departments, explaining what they do and how they work.

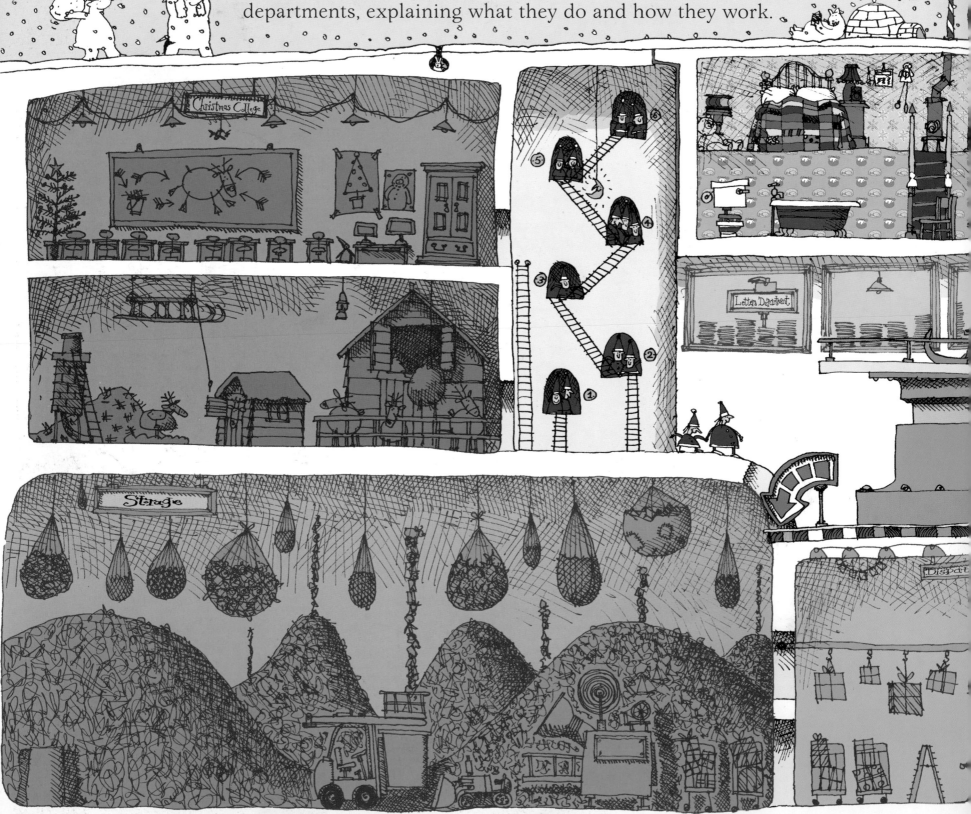

Who helps Santa?

Santa has many helpers. Most of these are elves. Elves live all over the world, but when they grow up, a lot of them get jobs with Santa and move to the North Pole. Each year more elves are recruited. The new elves must undergo extensive training before they start work. This is done at the CCE,* the school where they learn all about Christmas. First the elves take a general class called Christmas 101. Then they choose one of the many different courses available at the college. These courses teach them how to do a specific job in one of the departments.

* Christmas College for Elves

How does Santa know what you want?

In the months leading up to Christmas, children write to Santa to tell him what they want. This is a very good idea because if he doesn't know what you want, he will have to guess. Santa is probably better than anybody else at guessing what children want, but it really is worth sending him a letter.

Dear Santa, I would like a chocolate cake, some muffins, a jar of blueberry jelly, eight bars of chocolate . . . I wondered if you could get me a real working submarine? I know this is the fifth time I have asked for the same thing, but I really, really like socks. A blue bike would be fantastic, but if it is not possible, I would like a baby hippo. Yours sincerely, Ed

Dear Santa, I would like an alligator, a truck full of cakes and fifteen new pairs of sunglasses.
Love, John

Dear Santa, could you please send me a new brain so I could understand maths? If not, could you send me a go-cart and some paintbrushes? Thank you! Zach

Dear Santa Claus, is it possible to send me a very dangerous chemistry set and a set of flameproof clothes? Very truly yours, Grace

Dear Father Christmas, please see the attached list. I cannot wait till Christmas, so please forward all the presents to me right now. I shall expect them tomorrow. Most sincerely, Isabel

Dear Santa, I have been very good. Can I have as many pairs of socks as you can manage? I hear that lots of people don't like socks, so can I have theirs as well? I will be very happy, as I have a huge collection and I am always on the lookout for new and more interesting socks.
Yours faithfully,
Brian

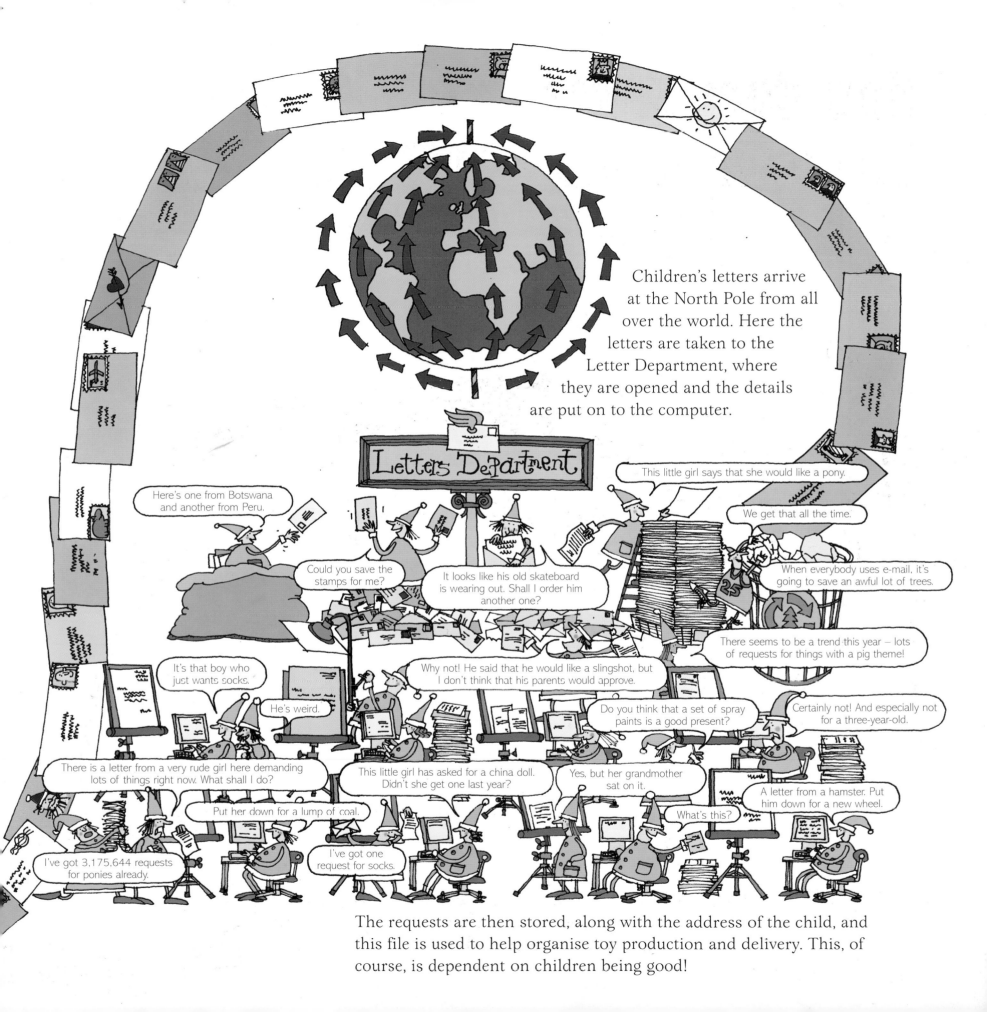

Children's letters arrive at the North Pole from all over the world. Here the letters are taken to the Letter Department, where they are opened and the details are put on to the computer.

The requests are then stored, along with the address of the child, and this file is used to help organise toy production and delivery. This, of course, is dependent on children being good!

Where are all the toys made?

The second section of the Toy Department is probably the most important part of Santa's world. This is the Toy Factory, or Production Department, as it is called. It operates around the clock – twenty-four hours a day, seven days a week. Elves work an eight-hour shift everyday. It is a good place to work, as the elves know the joy the toys will bring. They chat and sing and sometimes one of the elves will read stories to everyone over the public address system.

Where are all the toys kept?

Deep beneath the ice there is a gigantic cave where all the toys are stored. It is a magical place where mountains of toys cover many, many square miles of floor. Every toy that has ever been delivered by Santa has, at one time or another, been stored there. At the last count, that is over 976,592,331,684,078 toys.

Teams of elves who specialise in organisation separate the toys into piles. When orders come in over the address system, these elves fetch the toys.

Before the toys leave the Storage Department they are carefully wrapped up and labelled. Then they are sent to Dispatch.

Santa's Sleighs

scale 1/60

Santa has, in fact, two sleighs: one for long-distance work and the other for final delivery. These are built and maintained by the Transport Department elves.

Long-Haul Sleigh (for open country)

- aileron
- present sack
- Santa
- beard
- windshield
- helium bag
- helium bag
- helium bag
- helium bag
- elf
- fuel tank
- jet engine
- runners
- floatation deer

What happens then?

On Christmas Eve, at exactly 4:37 p.m., Santa sets off around the world. He starts in the east and works his way west, through all the time zones, picking up presents from the transporters when he runs low.

1. Set off from the North Pole

2. Deliver presents

3. Reload with presents

4. Deliver more presents

5. Repeat reloading and delivery

How does Santa get down the chimney?

Everybody thinks that Santa is very large, but in fact he is quite slim. Flying at high altitude in the middle of winter is very cold. He therefore wears a special heated suit. When he arrives at someone's home, he slips out of the suit and in via the chimney, door or window.

Santa has to be very flexible to get into some people's homes, so during the year he does lots of bending and stretching exercises (he is very keen on rock climbing and yoga). This keeps him fit and supple. He is in good shape for a man of his age.

Chimneys are easy, but I can get very dirty.

Windows are more difficult.

I have to practise for doors every day.

What do Santa and the elves do on Christmas Day?

They have a Party!

And then they go to bed . . .

for a while. . . .

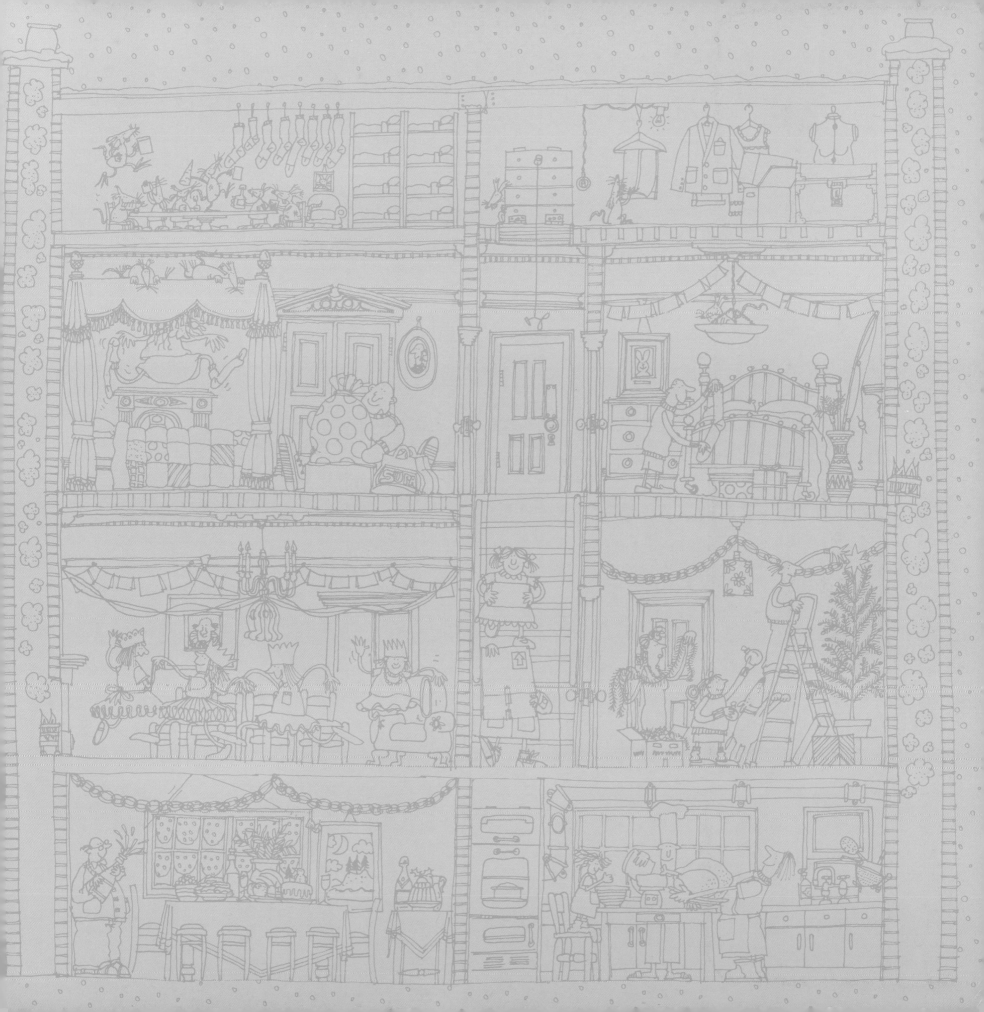